Moosetache

Margie Palatini

illustrated by Henry Cole

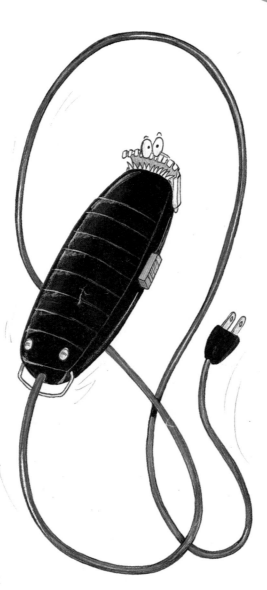

Hyperion Books for Children
New York

Text © 1997 by Margie Palatini.
Illustrations © 1997 by Henry Cole.

Printed in the United States of America.

First Edition
1 3 5 7 9 10 8 6 4 2

The artwork for each picture is prepared using acrylic paints and colored pencils.
This book is set in 16-point Meridian.
Book design by Edward Miller.

Library of Congress Cataloging-in-Publication Data
Palatini, Margie.
Moosetache / Margie Palatini ; illustrated by Henry Cole. — 1st ed.   p.   cm.
Summary: A moose's moostache is too big to control until he meets Ms. Moose, who has her own hair problem. They conquer each other's heart and their hair problems.
ISBN 0-7868-0306-1 (trade)—ISBN 0-7868-2246-5 (lib. bdg.)
[1. Moose—Fiction. 2. Mustache—Fiction.] I. Cole, Henry, ill. II. Title.
PZ7.P1755Mo   1997   [E]—dc20   96-26256

To my "dear" with the five o'clock shadow
—M. P.

To Dan, Caroline, and Jim, with love
—H. C.

oose had a problem.
A horrible, hairy, prickly
problem. It grew right below
his nostrils and just above
his upper lip.

A moosetache!

Now, not a few spare hairs or shy little stubble. No mere weak wandering whiskers on the upper lip of this moose. **No sirree!**
Moose had a big, bushy, bristly, mighty **moosetache**.
But a **moosetache** that was a burly, surly, mangy mess.
And it itched.

A lot.

Sure, he plucked.
And he tweezed.
He even clipped, snipped, and teased.
But his combs were still cowards.
And his brushes rebelled.
His scissors simply surrendered.

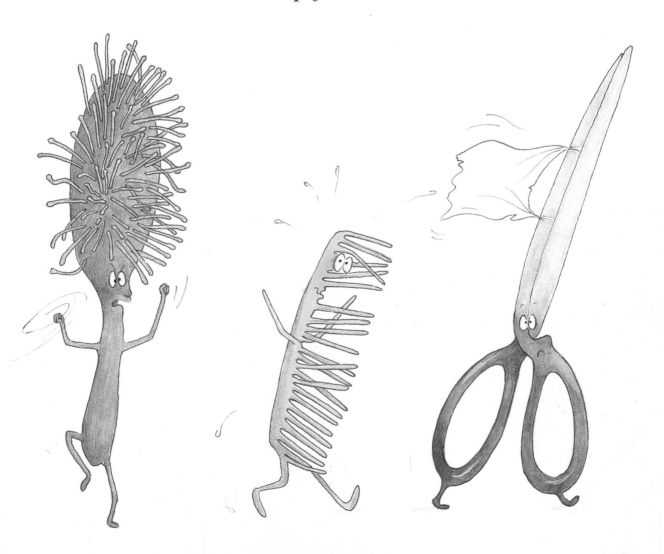

Moose was in a frizzy tizzy.
The **moosetache**
was completely
crimping his style.

He was a great hoofer. But
he could barely bop and hip-hop
with a **moosetache** going flip-flop.

He was a wonderful chef. But he simply could not
flambé his soufflé with all of those whiskers in his way.

And he was a daring skier. But how could he downhill race with the mighty **moosetache** blowing in his face? Moose had to do something—and soon.

But what?

After days and days of much serious thought, Moose
got an idea.

He crossed some hair here.

He crossed some hair there.

And he tied his **moosetache** around his neck.

A **moosescarf** seemed to be the ideal answer
to his problem.

It was so simple. So easy. So perfectly perfect.

But then . . . his **moosetache** got knotted . . . and mangled . . . and horribly tangled. And those hundreds of hairs still prickled and tickled.

Worse, Moose could barely take a breath with all that **moosetache** wrapped around his neck.

So,
Moose
untied,
unwrapped,
unknotted, and—
"aahhhh!"
—gulped in some fresh air.

He got another idea.

He parted some hair this way.

He parted some hair that way.

And he heaped all that **moosetache**
on top of his head.

Moosetachioed antlers seemed
to be the ideal answer to his problem.

It was so simple.

So easy.

So perfectly perfect.

Until . . . a squadron of squirrels
and one very nosy gopher
moved right in to the
Moose Motel.

They huddled and horded.

Furrowed in.

Burrowed out.

Needless to say, it
became quite crowded
up there on Moose's head.
And **heavy**.
And messy.

And very, very noisy.

The squirrelly chitting and chatting, squeals and squawks woke Moose every morning before the crack of dawn. And that gopher was giving the moose one hairy headache.

Moose needed his sleep.

He needed his rest.

He needed his **privacy!**

Moosetachioed antlers? **"Nuts!"** said Moose. So he unparted and unpiled, untwisted and untwined, and said **adios** to the hairy horns.

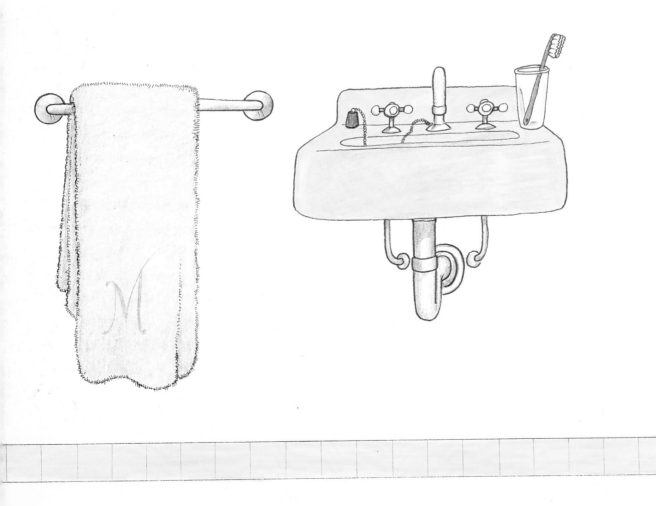

But now what? **What? What? What?**
The miserable moose took hold of a hunk of hair
and he wrestled it.

Then roped it.
He tethered, tied—
tamed!

Aha!
A
moosetail!

Now, *that* was so simple. *That* was so
easy. *That* was . . . not so perfectly perfect.

Talk about a **dizzy do!** Moose didn't know
if he was coming or going.

Backward? Forward? This way? That?

He didn't know which end was which.
Moose had to bail on the tail.

And so he thought. And thought. And thought some more. But no other idea was a worthy winner.

Braids were a bother.

A **moosetache**
sweater? . . .
Too sweltering.

Poor Moose! His problem was truly terrible.
Unbearable. Just downright sad.
He felt so alone. He didn't know what else to do.

Then, call it fate, call it destiny (it was probably dumb luck), but one day Moose tripped on his **moosetache** and just had no time to duck. **Oommf!**

"Pardon me, pardon me," they both said as they bumped.

Then they blinked.

And they stared.

And their hearts went

thumpa-thump.

She was a moose
with a bouffant so bodacious, outrageous—
well, it was just plain old **BIG!**
Hair after hair piled higher than high.
A skyscraping **do** of glorious curls.
A tower of swirling twists and twirls.
She was simply splendid, stupendous,
absolutely **superb!**

Of course Moose had to ask how she did what she did to get such a "**do**."

Ms. Moose winked and then whispered, "Just a little **glue**."

So . . .

She helped he—fearlessly plunge a hoof into a fat pot of the white gooey goop. And carefully, oh so carefully, they glopped. And they plopped. They pasted and they pressed. They coaxed and curled every truly unruly wayward whisker.

Around and around they tweaked and twirled those horrible hairs until Moose's once-mangy mess . . . was now a wondrous winding wave of marvelous **moosetache!**

Moose gazed in the mirror and smiled a broad moosey smile. He was so happy, so glad, just giddy with glee. He looked dashing and handsome.

Moose gushed, "Is that really **me?**"

With not a care
for one hair, the
moose pair **boogied**
and **bopped.**

They skied downhill.

Even uphill.

So, of course, it wasn't long after, that Moose and his **moosetache** and his beautiful bride fox-trotted and tangoed and waltzed down the aisle.

Good hair days.

Bad hair days.

They vowed to love and to cherish.

And with hearts heaped with love, and pots filled with goop . . . they both sighed, **"I do—glue,"** and promised never to part.

It was so simple. So easy. So perfectly perfect.

And—**it stuck**.